Secret Seahorse

Barefoot Books, 2067 Massachusetts Avenue, Cambridge, MA 02140

Text copyright © 2004 by Stella Blackstone. Illustrations copyright © 2004 by Clare Beaton
The moral right of Stella Blackstone to be identified as the author
and Clare Beaton to be identified as the illustrator of this work has been asserted

This book was typeset in 24pt Goudy Infant Regular. The illustrations were prepared in antique fabrics
and felt with sequins, buttons, beads and assorted bric-a-brac. Graphic design by Barefoot Books, Bath
Color transparencies by Jonathan Fisher Photography, Bath. Color separation by Bright Arts, Singapore
Printed and bound in China by Printplus Ltd
This book has been printed on 100% acid-free paper

ISBN 978-1-84148-937-7

Library of Congress Cataloging-in-Publication Data

Blackstone, Stella.
  Secret seahorse / written by Stella Blackstone; illustrated by Clare Beaton.
    p. cm.
  Summary: A sea horse leads the reader past coral reefs and underwater
creatures to a sea horse family hidden in a cave. Includes notes on
coral reefs and various marine animals.
  ISBN 1-84148-937-9 (pbk. : alk. paper) [1. Sea horses—Fiction. 2.
Coral reefs and islands—Fiction. 3. Coral reef animals—Fiction. 4.
Marine animals—Fiction. 5. Stories in rhyme.] I. Beaton, Clare, ill.
II. Title.
  PZ8.3.B5735Se 2005
  [E]—dc22
                                    2004017899

11 13 15 17 19 20 18 16 14 12

Secret Seahorse

written by Stella Blackstone

illustrated by Clare Beaton

Barefoot Books
Celebrating Art and Story

I saw a secret seahorse deep down in the sea.

I tried to swim beside him. He was too quick for me.

He swam past reefs of coral, with colors flower bright.

He swam past flickering fishes, then disappeared from sight.

I asked the octopuses where he might have gone.

They just shrugged and shook their legs. I steadily swam on.

I came across a mermaid, as she combed her hair.

I found an ancient shipwreck, but couldn't see him there.

At last I found a secret cave! It looked so dark and dim,
I stayed outside and shivered. I did not dare go in.

Then, in the cave I saw a glint, and guess who greeted me?

Not just one secret seahorse — a whole seahorse family!

Coral Reefs

Coral reefs are wonderful underwater worlds of their own.

The reefs are millions of years old and grow very, very slowly. One inch of coral takes nearly 100 years to grow!

Thousands of colorful fish and plants live in coral reefs. Although coral looks like a rock it is really a great colony of living creatures which feed on tiny animals, floating in the sea, called zooplankton.

The largest coral reef is the Great Barrier Reef in Australia.

Coral can only survive in saltwater that is clear, warm and clean with lots of sunlight. In many parts of the world, the coral has been killed because the sea in which it lives has been poisoned with all kinds of pollution like chemicals, sewage and fertilizers.

When a coral reef dies, all the fish that live in it have nowhere to live and they too disappear.

Turn over the page to find out more about the creatures that live in and around a coral reef.

Creatures of the Coral Reef

Anemone
Anemones look like pretty flowers. They catch their food using the poisonous stingers on their tentacles.

Angelfish
Angelfish have flat bodies which help them squeeze through tight places to escape from fish that want to eat them.

Barracuda
Barracuda are called "tigers of the sea" because they are fierce hunters with razor-sharp teeth.

Clown fish
Clown fish always live near anemones and help the anemones to keep their tentacles clean.

Crab
Crabs have five pairs of legs, with a big claw on the front ones. They can move in any direction, but they usually move sideways.

Giant clam

Giant clams live in the South Pacific and Indian oceans. The largest are as big as 4 feet long and weigh more than 500 pounds.

Hermit crab

Hermit crabs live in shells to protect themselves or their soft bodies. When they grow too big for one shell, they find a bigger one to move into.

Jellyfish

Most jellyfish catch their food with their stinging tentacles. Many jellyfish can give humans painful stings.

Lion fish

Lion fish are quite lazy and often just float about, waiting for their dinner to swim up to them. They use their long, sharp spines to kill.

Lobster

As well as scuttling, lobsters can swim backward by making big scooping motions with their body and tail. Most lobsters are a dark greenish color, but some are blue.

Octopus

When they sense danger, octopuses hide in rocky crevices or shoot out dark ink that clouds the water and gives them time to escape. Octopuses are very clever.

Oyster

Oysters live in shallow beds in warm ocean waters. The great pearl oyster, which makes the best pearls, lives in warm tropical seas.

Parrotfish

Parrotfish have powerful cutting-edge beaks. They are very popular in Hawaii, and at one time, only the royal family were allowed to touch them.

Sea slug

Many people think sea slugs are the most beautiful of sea creatures, as they come in all colors and patterns.

Sea turtle

Sea turtles live a long time. They swim enormous distances to lay hundreds of eggs on special beaches.

Sea urchin
Sea urchins are covered in tough spines. The spines protect them and are also used to dig burrows.

Shark
Sharks are even older than dinosaurs. They are found in seas all over the world, and can be very dangerous to humans.

Starfish (or Sea star)
Starfish have an eyespot at the very end of each arm. They use these to see light and movement.

Stingray
Stingrays whip their long tails to hurt their enemies. Their tails are covered in poisonous spines, which can kill humans.

Swordfish
The swordfish's "sword" is actually just an extension of its upper jaw. It uses it to skewer fish to eat.

Secrets of Seahorses

Seahorses are small fish that have armored plates all over their bodies. They move slowly by fanning their delicate fins.

They live in seaweed beds in warm water, hiding from larger fish.

Some are very small and are only an inch high, while others are one foot high.

Seahorses can move each of their eyes in different directions, making it easy for them to spot food.

They suck up food through their snouts, like sucking through a straw.

Seahorses are the only fish with tails that can hold onto things. They use their tails to cling onto sea-grass, coral or each other.

Female seahorses produce eggs, but it is the male who keeps them in a pouch in his body until they hatch after 40 to 50 days. They can have up to 400 babies at a time!

Male seahorses are the only males in the world who become pregnant like this.